I0598914

Tales For

Halloween

Volume Two

By Michael Gideon

Edited by Aaron

Conaway

A K&Q Press Publication

Front Cover Art by Aaron Conaway

First Edition 2022

All rights reserved. No part of this book may be reproduced in any form or by any electronic or mechanical means without written permission from its publisher. The characters and events in this book are fictitious. Any similarity to real persons, living or dead, is purely coincidental and not intended by the author.

Books by K&Q Press

The Timberhaven Chronicles

Before the Weaver

Waking the Weaver

Monsters in the Park (Coming Soon!)

The Michael Gideon Collection

Tales for Halloween

Tales for Halloween vol 2

Books by New Vison Comics Collective

Harrowed Earth Pentalogy

Book One: Appalachian Blues

Book Two: Cicero Wants You (Coming Soon!)

Table of Contents

Preface

Michael Gideon authored 39 horror novels, including *The Cage*, *What Waits in Dreams*, *Karnov's Clock*, and a wide array of short stories and poems.

He disappeared in the summer of 2010.

Editor's Note:

By all accounts, Halloween was Michael Gideon's favorite holiday. He had penned various story tributes to the monsters that were his favorite as a child. Multiple stories he wrote take place on or around October 31st, and star, in so much as he used their first names, close friends, and loved ones

(which is why you'll see the names of heroes/heroines/villains sometimes repeated in these Halloween-themed reprints.)

In the 70s, Mr. Gideon was interviewed on the radio series *Psychonaut Sessions*, a weekly series devoted to mysterious phenomena, by occult superstar Simon Myth. After the conversation turned to Mesopotamian folklore, *Edimmu* is the story born of that meeting.

According to lore, *12 Days* comes to us from a bet born of too much champagne at a Christmas function attended by Lovecraft biographer J.J. Thrashden and Michael. Sources at the party stated that Mr. Thrashden and Mr. Gideon bet each other that they could be the first to finish a

Lovecraftian-inspired Christmas tale. As Mr.

Thrashden's never saw print, so far as this editor

could find, I'd say Mr. Gideon won the bet.

We here at K&Q Press share in Mr. Gideon's love

of All Hallows Eve, and we hope you all hear

bumps in the dark, get woken by spectral voices

from the basement, and are disturbed by unseen

presences in your shower.

<u>Sour Mutters</u>

Few ventured into Winter Wood.

Every villager, from childhood, knew the stories of those who crossed into that shadowy forest. Legends grew in the telling of demons, angry spirits, unseen observers, and strange noises.

Of monsters.

Fear would not take Thatcher Drummond, however. At thirty-five, nearly an old man in those days, Thatcher singlehandedly hunted Winter Wood for the good of the village, keeping their larder filled in preparation for New England's harsh winters.

"I'm charmed!" he was fond of saying, "No evil thing, neither living nor dead, dares bar my path there. Winter Wood holds no fear for me!"

Until the winter of 1738.

Two weeks before the snow arrived, rats had infested the larder, devouring the village's source of life in the harsh cold.

Thatcher looked at it as a challenge.

"I'll go this very morning into the woods. I'll see to our survival."

Gathering his equipment and accompanied by his faithful hound, Beauregard, Thatcher made off into Winter Wood, whistling a tune as he went and promising to return by day's end.

Three days went by. Thatcher had not returned.

Natalie, Thatcher's sister, convinced herself
that she would go into Winter Wood and look for
her brother. She called a meeting with the village
elders to get their blessing and to see to it that
someone looked after her and Thatcher's place
while she went to find her brother.

"I'll come with you." Benjamin, the
blacksmith's apprentice, spoke up. Natalie thanked
him and turned to leave.

"As will I." Josephine, the wife of the town
drunk, said, standing up.

Confused but happy for the extra support,
Natalie agreed, and the trio left for Winter Wood.

The forest was cold as they entered, the bite
of the cold on exposed flesh only heightened by the
smell of dried, dead leaves on the forest floor. The
noise of their footsteps was the only sound to be

heard; the small group tightened their cloaks about them as they warily wandered down the only path they could make out.

Hours passed.

Natalie could feel someone watching her. She turned her head quickly, trying to catch whatever was at the corner of her eye. She saw nothing.

Josephine's eyes darted back and forth, scanning the wilderness before her for a sign of Thatcher. He was always kind, Thatcher. Not like some of the other villagers who mocked Josephine for being married to a drunk. When Thatcher smiled at her, she felt warmth spread through her. That warmth was why she kept the things that she and Thatcher did—in the dark, in the hidden—a secret.

Benjamin halted the group as they reached a creek, flailing his arms out to his side and stopping short, his eyes locked across the ice-filled brown water.

"The Lost Sisters," he whispered.

There, at the water's edge across from the trio, stood two young girls. Only, not girls. They were pale with moldy, peach pit eyes, set too far apart on their faces, and dirty rat teeth smiles that chittered. Their too skinny arms twitched as they twisted their heads on too spindly necks like confused dogs, staring at the travelers.

Watch for the little one. She bites.

"Who was that!?" Natalie screamed as she looked at the madness across from her.

"Who was who?" Josephine turned, asking Natalie.

"I—I heard someone. A whisper."

Benjamin turned to Natalie for a moment, but the Lost Sisters were gone when he turned back.

"Sour Mutters," he said, still looking across the creek, "Voices. Whispers without bodies. They mimic what they've heard here. Try to ignore them. No good can come from listening."

They walked on as the path in front of them gradually disappeared. Then, deciding to make camp, each ate their provisions quietly. Natalie kept first watch, sitting by the fire and praying for her brother's safe return from those wretched woods.

See you.

Natalie prodded the fire, trying desperately to listen to anything beyond the Sour Mutters.

Hiding, waiting.

Hungry.

Josephine dreamed.

She was back in the village in the dream, just outside Benjamin's cabin. She could hear someone speaking in an angry voice.

"*You* know. Everyone knows. One mustn't walk in Winter Wood."

In her dream, Josephine peeked into the window of Benjamin's cabin, seeing a young, beautiful woman standing before a roaring flame in the fireplace.

"But I allowed him passage," the woman continued, fuming, "to be the hero of his village, to feed you all, because he said he was mine. That we belonged together." She pulled a burning log from the fire with her bare hand and turned toward Benjamin, who, in Josephine's dream, lay asleep in his bed, "He lied."

As she watched the woman walk toward Benjamin, the flame on the log growing bigger, brighter, Josephine tried to wake up. She didn't want to see what was about to happen. Couldn't see it. Wouldn't see it. She just wanted to wake up. Benjamin screamed in her dream as the flames danced about his face, his hair. The fire was a living thing, carving his flesh with burning, white-hot teeth. The woman laughed.

Josephine retched as the smell of Benjamin hit her and then woke up to find Natalie trying to shake Benjamin awake. He was screaming the same scream from her dream.

Finally, Benjamin lay silent, lifeless—smoke from an unseen source poured out of his eyes, nose, and mouth. Natalie sat dumbstruck over his corpse.

It was then that Josephine saw Thatcher. He was looking at her from just outside the firelight. He looked lost. Confused. He turned to stumble away into the night.

"Thatcher!" Josephine shouted, running into the woods after him.

"Josephine, wait!" Natalie turned from Benjamin's body as Josephine stepped out of sight into the dark.

Josephine ran toward shadows that looked like Thatcher, only to turn and see him lumber off in a different direction by the light of the moon. If she could just catch him. Just get him home. She heard Natalie shouting her name but dismissed her. She would save Thatcher on her own.

Within minutes of leaving the fire's light and with no moon to see by, Natalie had completely lost

Josephine in the forest's shadows. She continued screaming after her in a vain hope that she could call Josephine back but to no avail.

Natalie was alone in Winter Wood.

Josephine followed Thatcher by the full moon for what seemed like hours as he stayed just out of reach. Finally, they came upon a rock face and, in it, a cave. Josephine could make out firelight as it danced within, and she watched as Thatcher stumbled inside.

"We'll get warm in the cave," Josephine thought, "I've saved him!"

As she stepped into the cave, Josephine saw a woman sitting with her back to Josephine, warming herself by the fire. She didn't know how, but she knew this was the woman from her dream.

"Come in, child," the woman said, her voice cold now, ancient, "warm yourself."

Josephine looked around the small cave. The rock walls were covered in red, covered in meat.

"Yes," the woman spoke again, "he said we belonged together. He said he was mine. But he lied. He laid with another. He laid," the woman spun around, "with YOU!"

Josephine's scream echoed into the night.

Bowwrow!

"Beauregard!" Natalie yelled, hearing her brother's dog just through the trees. "You're never far from Thatcher! Thatcher!" She screamed into the moonless night, "Thatcher!"

Bowwrow!

Natalie ran toward the sound of Beauregard's baying.

"Thatcher! Beauregard!" she tripped, uncaring as she hurried through the trees.

Bowwrow!

Natalie came into a clearing suddenly. She could hear water. Suddenly she felt hands all over her, pulling her down as she screamed. Chittering rat teeth sank into her face.

Watch for the little one. She bites.

The Court of Lesser Fiends

October brings encouragement,
Beside autumnal sights and scents,
A clarion call,
Understood by all,
Who seek bonfire's merriments

The embers paint the forest rich,
Shadows smudged orange, yellow, and pitch,
The sick oak was fell,
And positioned well,
Between the creek and narrow ditch

Revelers came to party there,
Their hoods drawn tight against night air,
All leaving their cars,
To dance 'neath the stars,
Heedless of what's watching from where

For eyes glimpse beyond the border,
Chaos flares against all Order,
Walls thin on this night,
With a scratch or bite,
To bring the world's reorder

'Twas Laurie who was first to spy,
No trick of light in corner eye,
Five in blonde tresses,
Glowing white dresses,
Little girls danced circles nearby

As Laurie witnessed this, scorning,
Her friend Ben yelled out a warning,
Then everyone saw,
All logic withdraw,
The air filled with wails of mourning

Ben's sis, Nancy, in her Ranger,
Saw by fire's light a Stranger,
Step from empty skies,
Summoned by the cries?
Lightning underscored the danger

The Stranger's chanting thus began,
Be it from woman or a man?
Then a green notion,
Its smoking potion,
Scattered party-goers all ran

Green smoke hid the stars in gritty,
The kids' escape wasn't pretty,
Making a line drive,
Down I-35,
Heading back to Kansas City

Nancy slid her truck into third,
Laurie and Ben said not a word,
Right in front of them,
A transparent gem,
The Stranger appeared almost blurred

Nancy couldn't lower her speed,
To account for the Stranger's lead,
But the Stranger fled,

Phased through to the bed
A bursting of sparks marked his deed

It punched through the back of the cab,
Coating them with glass from its jab,
Said, "I own this night,"
Robbed the cab of light,
And snatched Nancy out in a grab

Nancy's scared, to the Stranger begs,
Stares at its eyes of runny eggs,
It bent at its knee,
Unnaturally,
And bound her off on spindly legs

At once, Ben and Laurie could see,
In time to catch the Stranger flee,
With Nancy in arms,
That lacked human charms,
She screamed out a bloody "Help me!"

Laurie was first out of the truck,
Just as the street began to buck,
As Ben dove outside,
The unlucky ride,
Went under, down into the muck

Then the Stranger took Nancy down,
Where all the sewage went 'neath town,
In its raspy voice,
It said, "Here's your choice:
Stop here, or else follow and drown."

UNDERNEATH

Ben and Laurie made their way
Down
Through the rubbled road
Keeping pace with Nancy's echoed screams.
Phone flashlights dressed the sewer's stage.

A concrete path, two feet wide,
Kept Laurie and Ben clear of the
Fetid soup
Swirling at their feet.
Things breathed, skittering in the dark.
Carefully, so carefully, the duo tread,
Seemingly swallowed in the confines of the
Concrete throat
They found themselves in, when
Something disturbed the sewer's surface

A sharp fin sliced up through the
River of refuse
Swirling a preloved condom over
The stew of human flotsam
In its wake.

A hammer-shaped head explodes from the surface,
The shark's eyes, moldy nightmares;
Its sagging flesh long dead.
Laurie and Ben dive from its teeth as
The sewer wall envelopes them

IN BETWEEN

F a l l i n g.
.g n i l l a F
.sereht revo dna syadretsey otni dezispaC
.yb dessap sngis dna slobmyS
?G&B ?ereh saw 81-5-61-9-41-12-01
,ylnedduS
.hguorhT
Through.

INNER SANCTUM

Sconced torches surround the room,
Where they'd stumbled out, a tomb,
Nancy's tabled, bound at her wrist,
"Untie me!" she screamed loud, pissed.

Light glowed, showing upper levels,
Where dwelled monsters, ghosts, and devils,
For this is where the Night convenes,
Amidst the Court of Lesser Fiends

If there were any doubts who led,
That assembled horde of undead,
Seated above the dog with rabies,
A trio of vampire babies

VAMPIRE BABY #1
"Be silent, fleshlings,
Before this magnanimous
Council, lest we feed."

23

The eyes of the vampire babies flared
Golden purple,
Their voice-noises echoing like skittering
Cockroaches in the minds of the teens.
Ben's nose bled as he screamed, "They're in my
head!"

VAMPIRE BABY #2
"It was duly warned,
And so, is offered freely.
Sovereignty claimed."

Ben's rag doll body hit the floor,
Nancy, enraged, screamed out once more,
Laurie balked, torn between her friends,
There, for them, the night's horror ends

VAMPIRE BABIES #1 and #3
"The decision's sound.
We, the Court of Lesser Fiends
May now stand adjourned."

The Stranger bowed, both deep and fast,
Its function met before the caste,
And then the teens rise,
With gold/purple eyes,
All free to walk the earth at last.

<u>Edimmu</u>

October 30th

Great Basin Desert

11:43 p.m.

"Okay, wait. Do you mean, like, *28 Days Later* zombies or Romero's?" Bobby asked as Utah wind blew in through his open car window.

Sarah shifted gears in their road-abused SUV, then flicked her cigarette out the window as they sped down the highway.

"Both," she replied.

"Oh, god." Bobby said, picturing all that undead flesh, "I guess—wait, can I have a shotgun instead of a 9mm?"

"Sure, but that means your car only has a quarter tank of gas." Sarah smiled.

"Fine. Well, I guess I'd blast my way out of the—this is stupid. No *way* would I have gone to the library during a zombie apocalypse!"

"You hadn't heard the news," Sarah said after thinking for a second.

"Then why the hell would I be wandering the streets with a shotgun?" Bobby asked incredulously, "What kinda scary-ass library is this?"

"Yeah," Sarah admitted, "I didn't think this question through very well. My brain's getting tired." She said through a yawn.

"Well, we've been playing since Vegas. We can take a break." Bobby said, rolling his window up, "Want me to drive for a bit?"

"Sure," Sarah said, pulling over to a stop on the side of the highway. "Just let me get a few hours sleep, and then I'll take back over. We're still roughly ten hours out from home, according to the GPS. Heikes is probably already there."

For the first time since the siblings had started their road trip, Bobby's face didn't fall at the mention of Heikes' name, which Sarah took as a good sign.

While Sarah came around from the driver's side, Bobby got out of the SUV and stretched, looking up at the desert moon. The air had gotten chilly with the disappearance of the sun.

"I'm going to get in my bag quick, grab my sweatshirt," Bobby said, opening the door to the back seat as Sarah bent over to touch her toes, trying to get the blood flowing back into her legs.

"Okay. Check on Joe Pesci while you're at it?"

Joe Pesci was Sarah's pet guinea pig whose kennel was currently belted safe as houses in the back seat. Bobby reached in and gave his orange and white fur a gentle scratch between the ears, causing Joe Pesci to sort of shimmy with delight.

"He's fine," Bobby said, reaching for his bag.

"Hey, grab him a—"

"Grab what?" Bobby asked, looking up. He gave a sharp inhale when he saw what had interrupted Sarah's thought. What looked to Bobby as a large, black dog was standing in the light from their headlights, staring at them. "Is that a wolf?" Bobby whispered.

"Get in the car and shut the door," Sarah whispered back as she climbed into Bobby's now

vacant front passenger seat, following her own
advice.

Bobby hopped into the back seat and
slammed the door.

"*Is* it a wolf, Sarah?"

"Do they even *have* wolves in the desert? I
have no idea." Sarah said as the creature moved
closer to the front of the car, staying in the
headlights. "It looks hungry."

"Sarah, let's just go." Bobby shook her
shoulder.

"Yeah, that's a good idea." Sarah climbed
over the middle console back into the driver's seat,
"I'm wide awake now."

"Shit!" Bobby grabbed Sarah's arm,
"Where'd the wolf go?"

Sarah peered through the windshield but didn't see the wolf anymore. It wasn't in front of them or on the driver's side. "I don't see it. Is it over there?"

"I don't see it anywhere," Bobby said, peering back and forth through the window.

The animal, whatever it was, had simply vanished into the night.

"Let's go." Sarah shivered. She told herself it was because she was cold.

Sarah got them going down the highway again. They sat in silence for a long while, both lost in thought. Eventually, Bobby dozed off. As he slept, he dreamed.

He dreamt of long pathways cut in the sand and framed in stone. Something was chasing him. He could hear his heart beating faster; his breathing

30

heavier. Only, it wasn't his breathing. It belonged to whoever hunted him. It was close.

Closer.

Bobby came to a cliff in his dream. There, at the cliff's edge, stood his pursuer. A black wolf with an oddly human face. As the wolf with the man's face circled Bobby, it spoke:

"Lu eribu, wardum."

And then it jumped at him.

Bobby woke up screaming.

Sarah shook him by the arm.

"Are you okay?" Sarah asked.

"Yeah." Bobby grabbed the bottle of water from his cup holder and took a swig to steady himself. "I'm good. Bad dream."

"Sounded like it." Sarah said, "Well, we're almost in the clear. Twenty-four more miles, and we're out of the desert."

Bobby sat quietly. He couldn't explain why, but something about being free from the desert made him feel fantastic. He felt like he could run a mile, hell, a marathon!

But the feeling did not last. Bobby needed more rest, it seemed. Much more. His eyes closed as his head laid back to sleep.

A smile came across Bobby's face then.

A smile that was not his.

October 31st

Halloween

6:30 p.m.

"Is this the one?" a man's graveled voice asked beneath a sleeveless, hooded sweatshirt.

"Yes," the young girl seated next to him answered. "This is the town the siblings were headed to when it found them." Her eyes opened wide, unfocused, giving her face a blank look. "It all starts soon."

The man nodded and pulled their beat-up truck to the side of the road, just outside city limits. Small towns off the beaten path like this one were the creature's favorite nest.

Putting the truck in park, the man turned off the engine. He grabbed the steering wheel firmly with both hands and closed his eyes. He breathed deeply, in through his nose, out through his mouth. His eyes, hidden beneath the hood of his sweatshirt, were closed tightly in meditation.

His prey was near. The hunt would end soon, one way or another.

Finally, he checked his side mirror to ensure no one was coming and opened his door. The dome light shone over deep scarring covering his massive arms from wrists to shoulders, as though his capillaries had all exploded once upon a time.

"I'll get the gear ready." He said and got out of the truck.

The young girl, Lauren, who was fourteen years old if a day, came out of her trance. She undid her seatbelt so she could reach for something from the backseat. Soon she hefted an old black duster into her lap. Lauren stared down at it, remembering briefly the day she met its owner, the hooded man who had no name, and so she took to calling him Dusty over the months that they'd hunted the creature together—named for that jacket. Then, finally, she got out of the truck and headed toward the man with her prize.

"Here, you must put your coat on before we enter town. Remember last time." she smiled innocently and handed it up to Dusty, who towered over her.

Taking the jacket, Dusty put it on, causing his hood to fall, revealing further scarring over his bald head and face. Then, he pulled the hood back up, covering himself.

"It was hot." was all he said.

"Yeah, I know," blonde hair framed Lauren's face. "I'm just looking out for you. So, what's the plan?"

"We nearly had it in the desert," Dusty explained as he filled a duffle bag with various weapons from the back of their truck bed camper: a shotgun, a box of shells for it, two loaded handguns, and a long, thin blade wrapped in scented cloth. "It'll be weak now; should stay easier for you to track. But we've got to hurry."

"I'm sorry I didn't see the wolf," Lauren said. "I can't sense animals like I can people and—"

"It's done." Dusty interrupted. "Neither of us could've known how that would play out—the odds of other people crossing the desert just then. Let's focus on the job at hand."

"Right, right," Lauren said, admonishing herself silently. She closed her eyes, trying to locate the place inside her mind that they needed to find the creature. That was *her* part of the job.

"It *is* . . . weak," Lauren said, finding the creature's dark atonal signature amidst a concert of universal frequencies, just enough to read it. "It feels different. I think—it's in the boy." She squinted harder at first and then opened her eyes in that faraway look that meant she was using her gift. That's what Dusty called it, her gift. The first person in Lauren's short life to call it such.

"Damn!" Dusty slammed the truck tailgate. "Already able to take a human?"

"Don't worry," Lauren held her hands outright, still entranced. "The wolf gave it enough strength to leap, but only just. They had a small pet?

Some animal in the car—which might've meant the end of the monster. Unfortunately, the boy fell asleep before the creature died in their pet."

Dusty loaded the shotgun. "Bad luck all around."

"Yeah, but if we hurry, we can still save the boy." Lauren came to, giving her head a little shake and readying herself for the battle ahead.

Dusty's attention never left the shotgun.

October 31ˢᵗ

Halloween

J.J.'s Garage

4:05 p.m.

"You think I sound 'perturbed'?" J.J. yelled into the phone. "Well, I sure as hell didn't break your truck down, but now I've gotta call my client, and she's gonna sound a different word. Asshole!" she yelled the last to a dial tone before slamming the phone down in its cradle.

"Problems, boss?" Jason asked from the door to her office.

"Tires are gonna be late," she answered without looking up from the stack of papers on her desk. "Something about a blown head gasket on the delivery truck."

"Yeah, well, sorry to pile on, but . . . ."

"What fresh hell." J.J. then looked up to Jason.

"Well, spit it out."

"It seems James' lunch break is finally over."

J.J.'s morning had started poorly and had gotten worse as it went. She'd had to reprimand James twice about coming into the shop under the influence. He was a good mechanic—maybe not as good as Jason, but beggars can't be choosy—and those were tough to come by lately, which is why he'd gotten a *third* chance to clean up his act. An unheard-of occurrence in J.J.'s worldview, yet here she was.

J.J. decided that there wouldn't be a fourth chance.

The *cling-cling* sound from out in the garage
meant that momentarily, at any rate, James was
being saved by the proverbial bell.

"Thanks for the heads up," J.J. told Jason.
"Go back to your bay. I'll handle James after seeing
who this is. Might be someone stopping by to let us
know the building's on fire."

"Boss." Jason nodded.

Squad Unit 217

5:20 p.m.

"Rory's a prick, that's all I'm sayin'," Irvin said, taking a sip of coffee to punctuate his point. "He got no business getting Sheriff's Deputy."

Irvin's partner, Anita, didn't necessarily disagree with Irvin's take on things, but she'd made her peace with Rory's promotion and drove the squad car while her partner vented. Again.

"You think maybe he's got dirt on someone in the department?" Irvin asked, getting excited. "Like maybe—"

"Unit 217, do you copy?" the radio crackled to life on the dash.

Happy for the interruption, Anita grabbed the radio. "Dispatch, we copy. Go ahead, Sherie."

"You two better get over to J.J.'s," came Sherie's voice again. *"A call came through but got disconnected. There's some kind of trouble over there."*

"We're on it," Anita said and lit the lights and siren.

Blake & Summers Building

Fourth Floor

100.3 FM

7:14 pm

Marcus' fingers flicked across his keyboard with a Master's speed, his eyes flitting around the screen as he typed in command after command. Only he and the new guy were in the small office.

"Look, Chris—can I call you Chris?" he asked of the younger man seated next to him.

"Well, I prefer Christopher," the younger man started.

"It's all about the attitude, Chris." Marcus continued. "You take what you're given, and you smash it back at these people. Callers should fuel the fire of whatever topic you're on that episode."

"Uh-huh," Christopher rolled his eyes. He noticed the elevator doors opening through the office's glass walls and watched as a couple exited. The woman was agitated about something, maybe by the man with her. Her boyfriend? Christopher wasn't sure but thought so. He'd seen them around the station before.

"And the FCC is just going to have to get over themselves when I'm King of the Airwaves," Marcus continued, unaware and uncaring that his audience was inattentive.

Eric had listened attentively to everything Tiffany had said, only momentarily distracted by their having to navigate the police tape and crowd of onlookers outside to get into the building, toting her binders and books.

It had been a long morning.

"I don't like it, Eric," Tiffany said. "Ayasha never misses a deadline for *Veritas*."

"I know, babe," Eric repeated. "Are you sure we should interrupt her with all of this, though?" He'd asked that already, too.

Their elevator door opened onto the fourth floor. Ayasha, who didn't go on until two in the morning, had come in for a business meeting with some ad reps. Eric was pretty sure things would not go well with the binders and books.

"Look, we're doing a live podcast at the Hemmingford barn tomorrow," Tiffany huffed as they made their way down the hall. "And Ayasha hasn't even looked over any of this research you did yet. She doesn't know that Mr. Hemmingford has forbidden us to ask about Mrs. Hemmingford, but that I think we should. And where are we gonna put the cameras to try and catch the unknown little boy that's said to reside in the upper loft?"

Alice Street

4:14 p.m.

Jaedyn held the leash wrapped around her left wrist, fairly expertly, she thought, while Pickles, the bane of her dog-walking-to-help-buy-her-new-car existence Shar-Pei, handled his business right there on the sidewalk. Her right hand was contending with Pickles' owner over the phone.

"Yes, Father John," she said. "I'll be in front of my mom's garage in fifteen. No, it's the one connected to the B&S building. Blake and Summers, right."

Jaedyn wondered if priests were even supposed to have pets, let alone devil dogs, while Pickles, his load lightened, doubled back to begin wrapping his leash around her legs.

"Pickles?" she sighed into the phone. "Oh,
he's his regular sweet puppy self."

Pop!

The formless void leaped from its host, landing in another lowly cockroach as its brother exploded into pulp. The walls were full of the next ride.

Pop!

The dark vapor leaped again. Insects lasted mere seconds, but a cockroach was all that had been nearby. It had needed to abandon its feeding of the manform before he felt the full measure of its bite, though it had left instructions for him to hide should it need him later.

Pop!

In its roach body, the creature skittered along, wrapped inside darkness that held no sway.

It didn't know fear. Not like the manforms did, in their squalid meat. But it knew exhaustion.

Pop!

It knew that it couldn't continue this course much longer. The strength it regained from supping on the manform was squandered on the roaches.

Pop!

It needed a larger host. Something warm-blooded could withstand the feeding longer.

Pop!

Ahead in the dark was a mouse: a plump mouse, well-fed within these walls. The creature could hear its heart racing. The mouse sensed the monster, though it did not recognize the sensation precisely.

Only that it felt like death was near.

Heikes took another pull from his pocket flask, humming a clip from the chorus of Alan Jackson's *It's Five O'clock Somewhere* before continuing.

"Look, I'm not saying that Rob Zombie's *Halloween* is horrible—"

"It sure the hell sounds like you are," the mechanic with *James* stenciled on his shirt said, taking the flask back from Heikes.

"Well, okay, yeah, I am," Heikes admitted. "But it's as though Zombie saw that Carpenter made a chocolate meringue pie. He could taste the excellent custard. See the egg whites whipped into a fantastic foamy top, all built into this delectable homemade crust. And it's like Zombie's takeaway was 'Pour cream in bowl. Apply heat.' It's ridiculous!"

"If you say so," James said. "Hey, I gotta go. I'm already late getting back, but thanks for breakfast." He gestured with the flask as he handed it back, now emptied of its contents.

"De nada," Heikes said, putting his flask back in his inside coat pocket hiding place.

"Pop your car by sometime; I'll give you a free oil change," James added as he walked away, a slight stagger in his step. "I'm just over there."

"Sometime." Heikes' eyes unfocused as he stared into the street. "Sure."

A dirty SUV pulled to a stop before him, and still, Heikes didn't blink. Finally, the driver honked to snap him out of his mental time-out.

"Hey, Heikes!" Sarah yelled from the driver's seat.

"Holy shit!" Heikes stood up, exiting his fugue state. He began blinking rapidly and took in a deep sigh as he looked at Bobby sleeping in the passenger seat of the SUV. "Jesus, Sarah, you guys made excellent time. Our boy's out, eh?"

Sarah popped the Unlock button so Heikes could climb in the back seat.

"Yeah, the jerk was supposed to drive the last leg so that *I* could get some shuteye, but—"

"Jesus!" Heikes yelped, staring through the open car door at what appeared to be an exploded fuzzy orange and white sock. Various chunks of viscera and other miscellaneous gore accompanied the shredded fur contained inside the kennel.

"What?" Sarah opened her car door and jumped out without checking for traffic. She ran around the SUV until she was stopped short by the scene of the once fluffy Joe Pesci.

In the screaming, neither Sarah nor Heikes saw Bobby get out of the SUV and head into the building behind them.

Blake & Summers Building

Fourth Floor

100.3 FM

7:18 pm

"So what we're saying," the out-of-town exec with the power suit began her closing sales pitch, standing before Ayasha from across the table, "is that *Ayasha After Dark* needn't stay an overnight show."

"Not that we're suggesting that it's not performing spectacularly—" chimed in a station lackey.

"Nobody's saying that *at all*." The out-of-town exec interrupted, taking her eyes off Ayasha for the first time that meeting to give the lackey an icy stare. She leaned over the table, looking back at Ayasha as though they were co-conspirators. "Numbers don't lie. But widen your gaze. Take in the bigger picture. We think you'd kill in Atlanta."

Ayasha took in a deep breath, then let it out. She did it again. The paperwork they'd given her before the meeting had a lot of numbers on it. Pretty big numbers, if she was honest. Life-changing figures.

"Well," she began. "You've certainly given me a lot to think about. Can I take a few days and—"

The door to the conference room swung open, banging into and leaving a crack in the glass wall. Tiffany came stomping in with Eric close behind her.

"What the hell?" the exec straightened up, fuming at the interruption.

"Look, I'm sorry," Tiffany said the first to Ayasha, the second to the exec. "This will just be a minute. Look," back to Ayasha, "I know you've got this meeting, and it's all important, but we've got a show to do tomorrow. Hemmingford, in case you forgot. And this is a big deal for us, which you used to care about, but now it doesn't seem like you do so much. First, we lost this year's Podkin Pie Award to Pop-Culture Bombcast—they don't even do horror-related material! And now—"

Tiffany's following words were drowned out in the sound of the room exploding around them. Fiery remnants of the floor hit the out-of-town lackey, shredding his body into a lung-diseased sneeze, while the concussive blast blew his boss through the window with such force that a rooftop worker would find her left leg below the knee

across the street a week later.

J.J.'s Garage

4:06 pm

Samantha's husband took a "there are no
dummy lights on, so everything's running
smoothly" approach to car maintenance, which was
to say he knew nothing about cars. However, she
knew the ticking she heard meant trouble, so
whether they could afford it or not, a trip to J.J.'s
was in order.

As Samantha pulled her car into the garage
and over a tell-tale hose, the *cling-cling* sound made
her smile.

"What can I do ya for, pretty lady?" a
mechanic who'd appeared at her car door asked.
The waft of his alcohol-infused breath accosted
Samantha's nose like a boxer on a speed bag.

"Uh," she coughed. "Is J.J. here?"

"James!" J.J. yelled, coming down the stairs from the upper office with Jason following behind. "Get upstairs. Now."

Nobody else said anything. Samantha wondered, growing nervous in the tension of the garage if maybe she should trust the lack of dummy lights and just drive a car that ticks.

"Well," James said, staring at J.J. and Jason. "It seems my services are needed elsewhere."

Blessed Unity Church

4:22 p.m.

Father John was running late to meet Jaedyn, which left him feeling rushed and caused him to all but run down the steps in front of the church.

It was not a feeling he enjoyed.

Someone was stealing the sacrament wine, though, and this he really could not abide.

Father John crossed the street double-time as though he might make amends for committing a traffic infraction if he did so quickly. His collar was wet with sweat as he came upon Jaedyn in front of her mother's garage.

Pickles was yipping and tugging at his leash, trying desperately to escape from the young girl as she, for her part, tried to comfort him.

"Pickles, come now," Father John tried to intercede.

"I don't know what's gotten into him!" Jaedyn explained. "He was fine on the walk over, but now he's lost his mind."

Father John knelt to his dog, stroking Pickles' head as he tried to comfort him. Pickles jumped into his arms. Father John could feel the poor animal's heart racing, its eyes bulging, staring back toward J.J.'s Garage.

A sensation went through Father John then; a cold wave ran from the base of his skull to the small of his back. Prickling, pins-and-needles with no motivation save one.

Fear.

Blake & Summers Building

Street

6:48 p.m.

Dusty jerked the truck to a stop, causing an impatient man behind him to blare a horn and loose a hand gesture.

There was the building they sought. The police on the scene were all the indication Dusty needed. This was the creature's new den, where it would build its strength back. Dusty nudged Lauren's shoulder, shaking her from her trance state.

"No need," Dusty said, pointing. He pulled the truck out of traffic, turning down a quiet side street.

"That was fast," Lauren said, peering through her window and trying to determine what had happened as they drove slowly around the building to the back. "It doesn't feel as though fast is good this time." She added, looking to Dusty as if she'd posed a question.

"It's not." Dusty agreed. "Grab your gear."

The duo each carried a backpack, and Dusty held the shotgun hidden under his duster. Police on the scene made this problematic. Hell, if he was being honest, the creature being in a city of this size was a nightmare. They'd have to work fast if they had any chance of finishing this.

A loading bay at the rear of the building wasn't crawling with police yet. Dusty knew what had happened inside seemed to be centered toward the front of the building, but that wouldn't last.

"We're clear there," Lauren pointed to the loading bay, telling Dusty what he already knew.

"The police are focused on the garage next door, mostly. There was," Lauren shuddered. "It was awful in the garage."

That Dusty hadn't known.

As the two entered the building through the bay door, Dusty took the position in front of Lauren, as he always did. And, like always, it made Lauren feel safe. Special.

If she could read Dusty's mind like she could other people, though, she'd realize that it was merely a strategy for Dusty.

You don't leave your strongest weapon unguarded.

"Oh my God," Sarah screamed again, her hand quivering toward the remnants of Joe Pesci. "What the hell happened?! Bobby, what could've—"

She saw that her brother was gone.

"It's like the little guy just . . . blew up." Heikes pointed out. A comfy blanket of cheap bourbon helping him to state the obvious.

"Where's Bobby?" Sarah asked. "Heikes, where's my brother?"

"I—" Heikes looked bewilderedly toward the building behind them. "You think he went inside?"

"Bobby!" Sarah yelled, looking up at the building. She ran toward the entrance.

"Hey, Sarah! What about your car?" Heikes wondered. "Guess I'll have to park it." He said when no answer came from his friend.

Blake & Summers Building

Inside The Walls

4:09 pm

The mouse contorted in pain. The creature within it knew there were seconds left before the inevitable explosion of flesh would leave it hostless again. It needed to move quickly, formulate a better stratagem, but a larger host would need to be unconscious for it to feed upon, and the manforms, while plentiful inside this building, stayed awake in the sun.

It took a brief second, one that it didn't have to spare, to locate its previous manform feeding trough. But, no, that host was too far away presently.

It drove further down the wall's innards as the mouse's side began to split.

J.J.'s Garage

4:12 pm

James knew that J.J. would calm down, cave, and let him keep his job if he could just get back to work. Get her mind settled on something else. Damned if he didn't have a strong buzz going, though.

"Sure thing, J.J.," he said, returning to his work bay. "Let me just get the Silverado done. Won't take two shakes." He picked the long handle to his floor jack up from the top of his toolbox and slung it over his shoulder.

Jason walked over and went to grab James by the arm. "Look, J.J. said to—"

Startled, James spun quickly, swinging the handle to his floor jack. It struck Jason in the side of the head, hard enough that the big man went down.

"Jesus!" J.J. yelled.

"Oh my God, are you all right?" Samantha said, getting out of her car.

"He was coming at me!" James explained. "You all saw!"

"He's out cold," J.J. said, checking Jason's pulse.

"I'm calling 911." Samantha dialed her phone.

"You tell 'em I was defending myself!" James dropped the floor jack handle.

"James shut the hell up." J.J. looked up at him. "You're done here, you hear me? Done. Pack your shit and get out of my garage."

"What? You can't—for this?"

Samantha covered her other ear to hear over the argument. "Yes, I'm at J.J.'s Garage, and there's been an accident. There's a man down and—"

Jason sat bolt upright so quickly that Samantha screamed.

"I feel amazing!" he said. He jumped up to his feet.

"Jason, take it easy. You were out—" J.J. took him by the arm.

"Nah," Jason said, walking over toward James, who was putting his hands up in an "I don't wanna fight" pose. "It was nothing."

"I—hold on just a sec," Samantha told the 911 operator, and she took in the scene.

"Still, maybe slow down." J.J. tried again.

"Yeah, I'll nap," Jason said, throwing a friendly smile over his shoulder to J.J. "Just one thing first."

James tried to speak, but Jason moved with inhuman speed, taking James by the throat and choking any words that had been coming.

"Jason!" J.J. ran to stop what was about to happen. She failed.

"You're just so rude," Jason began, slamming James down unto a workbench and holding him there. A car battery lay next to James' head. "And I feel as though we've had enough of you."

With his free hand, Jason picked up the car battery. He managed to land four blows before J.J. got to him. James' head had caved like an overly-ripe melon upon the first.

Samantha dropped her phone in stunned silence.

J.J.'s Garage

4:13 p.m.

The creature's psyche throbbed in rage within its meated walls. Fate had granted it life in a spectacularly fortuitous manner, only to have this ignorant manform squander away the opportunity to lie low and feed with an emotional outburst.

Eons of life, and it would need twice as long to understand humans.

Still, it continued to have a link with its former manform host as well. So maybe it could unite the two. Feed on both simultaneously to bolster its strength and increase its power.

With a little more focus, it may even be able to enslave manforms through their conscious minds. Just a touch more . . .

Tiffany came to slowly, her conscious mind emerging just behind a cough of smoke escaping her lungs. Her left hand rose to explore the wetness on her face and returned red with blood.

She wasn't sure if it was hers.

"Tiffany!" Eric was yelling from somewhere in the dark. Small fires scattered shadows among the smoke-filled air, and an alarm blared.

"I'm here," Tiffany started.

"Ugh," Christopher blanched from behind Tiffany. "Is that—oh my god, is that an ear?"

"Focus!" Marcus clapped his hands once, then pointed at Tiffany. "Help her up while I find the boss."

"You okay?" Christopher asked Tiffany before offering his hand.

"Eric!" Tiffany cried out, choosing to remain on the floor.

"Over there," Marcus was telling someone. Eric limped out of the smoke. He fell to Tiffany, and the two hugged.

"Are you okay?" Eric asked.

"I'll live. What the hell happ—"

"Somebody get this piece of shit off of me!" Ayasha yelled. Tiffany looked over and saw her friend's legs stuck under some debris from the ceiling.

Marcus and Christopher ran over and helped pull her out.

"Somebody talk to me," Ayasha said through gritted teeth, holding her limp right arm cradled in her left.

"We're stuck," Christopher barked. "The blast took out the elevator, and the stairwell is blocked by, well, explosion leftovers. And I don't know about your cell, but ours are—"

"We've got a plan, though," Marcus thumped Christopher in the arm. "Cops were already crawling around downstairs. I think we can rig up things in here through the system, try and get 'em on their radios. The north windows could make a serviceable exit."

"Get on it," Ayasha told them.

Blake & Summers

Streetside

5:25 p.m.

"REPEAT, OFFICERS IN NEED OF
IMMEDIATE BACKUP! WE'VE GOT A BODY
DOWN IN THE STREET AND SHOTS FIRED!
SHOTS FIRED!"

Rory radioed in to dispatch.

"Sherie, I'm just a few minutes out. I'll swing by on my way home."

While Rory wasn't sorry that he took the Sheriff's Deputy job, he *did* miss his beat.

"Anita and Irvin are en route already, Deputy." Sherie came back after a beat.

Yet another person who didn't think Rory had deserved the promotion, it seemed.

"I heard," Rory answered. "I patrolled that side of town for three years. I'm gonna check up. Over."

He put his radio back without waiting for a response and spun the car toward the Blake & Summers building.

J.J.'s Garage

4:17 p.m.

J.J. grabbed Jason's gore-soaked arm, making him drop the car battery onto the workbench.

"Jason, stop it!"

"Lu eribu, wardum!" Jason screamed into her face with such force that spittle frothed from his mouth.

"Wh-what?" J.J.'s world spun out as though someone had changed the channel on a show she'd been watching.

Jason roared, swinging a backhand that connected with the side of J.J.'s head, spinning her around and crashing into Samantha's front bumper.

It was this act of violence that shook Samantha back to the reality she'd escaped in witnessing the previous one. She made it to J.J. as Jason stretched his arms behind his back as though preparing to do some yoga.

"Sorry 'bout that, boss," Jason said, lolling his head back and forth in a relaxing neck roll. "I just feel so amazing!"

Samantha helped a bloodied J.J. to her feet.

"Let's get out of here," she told the likely concussed woman next to her. J.J. was staring as though she saw three of her.

"No," Jason said, snapping his attention toward the women. "I think not."

Blake & Summers Building

Second Floor

4:17 p.m.

"Bobby!" Sarah whispered harshly down the hallway, peering into any office that happened to be open as she walked by.

"First floor was a bust," Heikes explained, having caught up to Sarah. "Pretty sure the lobby attendant is gonna call the cops after all your screaming in front of the building and then running around inside."

"Did you move my car?" Sarah asked, ignoring him.

"Yeah. What the hell's going on with our boy?"

Sarah called Bobby's name again, a little louder this time.

"I don't know."

It was eerily quiet on the second floor, made up of business offices. The sound of Sarah's boots was all she could hear besides Heikes' labored breathing. The hustling seemed to be wearing on him.

Then, Bobby appeared from around the corner at the end of the hall.

"Bobby, Jesus man," Heikes began. "You're freaking us out."

Bobby walked toward them, still some thirty feet away down the hall.

"Heikes!" he said with a big smile. "Sarah, look! It's Heikes!"

"Bobby, what's the matter with you?" Sarah squinted at her brother, trying to read his face. She always knew what he was thinking, ever since they were kids. No poker face, her brother. Not with her. But now, something was different.

"Me?" Bobby asked. "Why, nothin' in the world's wrong with me. I feel awesome. Not like Daniel and Rebecca, though, eh Heikes?"

Heikes stopped walking, which made Sarah pause. Bobby was still coming, though.

"When you rolled Rebecca's car last fall, I mean." Bobby continued. "What'd you drink that night, fifteen beers?"

"Fuck you," Heikes whispered. His pulse quickened as Bobby kept walking their way.

"Fuck me?" Bobby's face rippled in fake shock. "Fuck them, you mean. Rebecca died quick, right? Thrown through the windshield, still passed out drunk. Never knew what hit her. Or, well, what she hit, I mean."

Heikes' clenched his hands into fists even as Sarah stuck her arm out to hold him back.

"Bobby, enough," she told her brother.

"But Daniel," Bobby continued, now some ten feet away. "In the backseat, Daniel did *not* die quickly. The roof of Rebecca's car sheared into pieces, and Daniel caught a shard, what, three feet long? Right through the right side of his face. His cheek was gone, his ear. His remaining teeth clinking on that metal as he was trying to ask you—what was it? 'Can you roll the window up, please?'. Because, as he bled out, slowly, half of him in what was left of the trunk and the other laying in his own lap, he was cold."

Heikes shoved Sarah aside, knocking her to the ground in his suddenness, and rushed Bobby. Quicker than Heikes could see, though, Bobby had moved, sidestepping the bigger man and tripping

him to the floor as well.

"No," Bobby said. "I think not."

J.J.'s Garage

4:23

"I don't know why the garage doors are shut," Jaedyn told Father John as she passed him Pickles' leash. "Let me just—"

"No!" Father John startled Jaedyn with his ferocity. "I'm sorry, it's just that, don't you feel it?"

"Feel what?" Jaedyn asked, looking at Father John through worried eyes.

"Something is wrong in there."

Jaedyn smiled politely but walked toward the garage. She'd practically grown up inside, with the smell of oil and gas. Greasy engine parts and special order paint jobs. This garage was Home.

"Nothing bad will happen. I won't be five minutes," Jaedyn told the priest.

She was wrong on both counts.

J.J.'s Garage

Street

6:50 p.m.

Rory took note of the old truck that slow-rolled behind the B&S. Something felt off. He excused himself from the paramedic who was dressing his wounded arm.

"Sir, you're still bleeding," she announced, as though it wasn't Rory's shoulder seeping blood down his back.

"You can finish in a second," he told her. He walked away from the carnage at J.J.'s Garage and into the five-story building next door, drawing his sidearm along the way.

Blake & Summers Building

First Floor

7:12 p.m.

Lauren held a baseball bat in one hand; it was the only weapon in Dusty's arsenal that she felt comfortable with and her little green flashlight in the other. Just in case the lights went out. She wasn't overly fond of the dark.

Dusty walked ahead, his long coat covering the loaded shotgun he was wielding. This was the night he killed the creature; he could feel it. Every step led toward their final confrontation.

The first floor was nearly clear.

He had taken two or three more steps before he realized that Lauren was standing still. He looked back for an answer only to find her holding her hand to her face.

Her nose was bleeding.

"It knows what she can do," a voice rang out from one of the empty offices around them. Dusty couldn't tell if the voice was from a male or female, but the owner was definitely under the creature's thrall. "And so, she must be removed."

Dusty brought his shotgun out from under his coat. The pretense was no longer necessary.

"You hope to eradicate such a beautiful life with such a mundane instrument?" The voice questioned. "You are too late. Lu eribu, wardum!"

Dusty laughed.

"Seems you're not strong enough to feed through sound yet," Dusty mocked the voice and thereby the creature.

"No need," the owner of the voice, a young man whose arms were blackened from exploded blood vessels, stepped from the last office on the left. He raised a handgun and pointed it into the office diagonal from him.

"Dusty, look out!" Lauren screamed. "He's going to—"

The first floor exploded.

Blake & Summers Building

Fourth Floor

7:18 p.m.

The creature hated losing a host, especially one that had served so well as the meatsuit that called itself "Bobby," but it had all but used what meager material Bobby had to offer. The manform would have diminished soon anyway.

It was so close to its goal! If only it could manifest into one more manform, it could regain enough of its former glory to feed off these cattle in its mother tongue.

So close.

But, at least the blast from the explosion had supplied a new host a mere twenty feet up. Now, if the creature could only keep this fresh host from acting on its baser instincts long enough.

Blake & Summers Building

West Stairwell

7:27 p.m.

Rory groaned, picking himself off the stairs. The explosion on the floor above came from the east side of the building, but the blast had still been forceful enough to knock him down the stairs.

He looked for his gun but couldn't find it by the low glow of the red emergency lights.

"Anybody read me?" he asked his shoulder radio.

Nobody answered.

Feeling woozy, Rory went on up the stairs to the first floor.

Upon opening the exit door, smoke filled the stairwell. Rory could hear the sirens of the firetruck that was en route.

"Anybody alive in here?" he asked, assuming he already knew the answer.

A low moan came from nearby.

Rory came around the corner, peeking around first to try and gauge the situation. A young blonde girl was only then starting to get up from under some rubble.

"Are you okay?" Rory asked, kneeling to the girl.

"Wait!" the girl tried to shout.

But someone had already kicked Rory in the side of the face, knocking him to the ground.

Sitting cross-legged on the floor, Christopher synched the backward-rigged motherboard to the cell he and Marcus had reconditioned.

"Try that," he told the older man.

Marcus beamed as power surged their game plan to life. He clapped Christopher on the shoulder.

"Well done, us!"

Then he picked up the chair he'd been sitting in, lifted it above his head, and smashed it down onto Christopher's.

"We did so amazingly!" Marcus yelped, jumping into the air and landing both of his feet onto Christopher, who was laid out cold from the chair blow, crushing the younger man's throat in the process. He then proceeded to kick the now lifeless body joyously.

"I just,"

Kick.

"Don't know,"

Kick.

"How we could be,"

Squelch.

"Any more,"

Squelch.

"Amazing!"

J.J.'s Garage

4:30 p.m.

Jaedyn was immediately concerned when she didn't see anyone on the drive. James not being around wouldn't have been a big deal, par for the course, actually, but Jason or her mom should have been up front.

"Mom?" she called up to the office. No one responded.

She walked around to the back of the garage. Sometimes, if they had a particularly busted car come in or one of her mom's wealthier clients brought in a hot rod, everyone would gather in the lot behind the building.

It was then that Jaedyn saw blood pooled in front of James' bay and on his workbench.

"Mom!" she screamed.

"Be. Quiet." some woman Jaedyn didn't know ordered at her from within an old Dodge van. "Get in here before I lock it again."

Jaedyn quickly jumped in through the open sliding side door just as the woman gently slid it shut behind her.

"What is going on?" Jaedyn asked. "What's all that blood, and where is my mom?!"

The woman shushed her and looked out through the van's back window into the garage.

"You've got to shut up," she said. "He'll hear us and come back."

"Who?" Jaedyn looked out the window as well.

"The mechanic, Jason. He killed the other one with a car battery. A freakin' car battery! Just lifted it and smashed his face."

Jaedyn couldn't make sense of any of the woman's words.

"James is dead? Jason killed James? Where is my mom!"

A lug nut wrench busted into the van's side window, causing both women to scream. Jason came running. He slammed into the van, rocking it roughly with his inhuman strength. Jaedyn looked at his face through the window. His eyes were purple where they should have been white, as though he'd burst every blood vessel in them.

"Little pigs, little pigs, let me in!"

Street Outside J.J.'s Garage

4:50 p.m.

Father John wasn't sure why he was still standing in front of the garage. Worry, he knew, Jaedyn was fifteen minutes longer than she said she'd be, but something else kept him there.

Pickles was going crazy, clawing at the sidewalk to get away until his paws bled. Father John finally walked him to the metal trash can across from J.J.'s and tied him there.

"It's okay, boy," he tried a soothing tone that he didn't feel. "I'll just be a minute."

As though he remembered what Jaedyn had said before entering the garage, Pickles howled a mournful wail as Father John walked back across the street.

The front entrance to J.J.'s Garage stuck a little when Father John pushed it open. Likely everyone enters through the usually open front garage doors, he thought, as Jaedyn had mentioned.

"Hello?" he called out to the silent dark.

"Hello." someone in the dark answered back. A cinder block caught Father John in the chest, breaking some of his ribs. Miraculously, he kept his footing.

"Our Father," he wheezed. Blood bubbled in his mouth. "Who art in heaven."

J.J. stepped out of the shadows, wild-eyed and coated in blood from what appeared to be a head wound.

"Go to sleep, Father," she said. "It will all go much easier if you just pass out."

Father John slid over, holding himself up on the front counter.

"Hallowed be thy n-name."

"Suit yourself," J.J. said, walking toward the holy man like a prey-cornering panther.

J.J.'s Garage

5:10 p.m.

Jason circled the van, hitting it with his fists now and again on a pass.

Samantha was finding it hard to breathe in the confines of the terrorized van. She'd never had trouble with claustrophobia in her life, but she didn't know what else this was. Maybe a panic attack.

She had plenty to be panicked about, after all.

Samantha looked at the phone in her hands, trying to will it to have bars.

"I think I can make it back outside," the young woman, J.J.'s daughter, said as she looked out the van's window toward a side exit. "Get some help."

"Don't be stupid!" Samantha snapped. "You'd never make it."

Jason banged into the van again.

"I'm going to go for it," Jaedyn said. "When he's at the front, I'm going out the back."

"No, wait, I've got a signal!" Samantha shouted.

Before Samantha could protest Jaedyn's plan further, Jaedyn was enacting it.

Jason slammed the Dodge's hood, which was Jaedyn's cue. She flung the van's back door open and sprinted across the garage, sparing a look back to see how close Jason was. Samantha's screaming was when it dawned on Jaedyn what had happened. Jason hadn't pursued her.

He'd gone after Samantha.

"Police! Help, I'm at J.J.'s Garage and—" Samantha pleaded.

Jaedyn looked in horror as Jason climbed into the back of the van. She saw him grab a handful of Samantha's hair. Mercifully, the backseat of the van blocked the rest of the episode from Jaedyn's view.

Sticking to her plan, she ran for outside. It was dark in the hallway that led out, but she could see the exit sign above the door.

She was going to make it.

But then the exit door swung open, and Father John stood there. He seemed to be struggling to stand upright, but there he was.

"My girl, even with these busted ribs, I feel great!" he exclaimed. "Try it!"

A heavy gear flew from Father John's hand, smashing Jaedyn in the face so hard that the entirety of her facial bones collapsed like eggshells.

"Oh my," Father John said. "I suppose that was much too hard."

It was the last thing Jaedyn ever heard.

5:19 p.m.

The creature fed, feeling its strength returning. Then it felt something else—a presence.

The hunter and his pet, the manforms the creature couldn't inhabit. They were close, mere miles and closing.

The hunter who had set traps for it, meaning to end its existence merely for being what it was.

Well, the creature could set traps as well.

It eyed the acetylene tanks in the corner.

J.J.'s Garage

Street

5:19 p.m.

Anita stopped and turned off the squad car's spinning lights. The street in front of J.J.'s was quiet like someone had hit a cosmic Mute button, save for a yipping dog that someone had left tied to a trash can across from the garage.

"Can you believe they let some people have dogs?" Irvin asked his partner, noticing her see the dog.

Anita gave a noncommittal nod, put her hand on her service gun, left it holstered, and walked toward the darkened garage's entrance.

"Ah, dammit," Irvin said.

Anita turned to see what drew her partner's attention. An unmarked car was pulling up next to them; its headlights pointed onto J.J.'s accusingly.

"Officers," Rory said, getting out of his car. "What's going on?"

"We just got here," Irvin grunted. "But we've got this."

"I know the layout," Rory said, walking in front of the beams from his car. His shadow stood twenty feet tall along the wall. "Let's do this by the book. I'll go around back. You two take the front."

Anita didn't see the point in arguing who did what and headed toward the entrance.

Irvin finally followed.

"Screw that guy with his pants on," he whispered to Anita. "Seriously, we can't handle a disturbance call?"

Anita pushed the front door to J.J.'s open with her left hand and drew her gun with her right. Rory showing up made things feel tenser for some reason.

"Police!" she announced. "Did someone call for help?"

Behind J.J.'s Garage

5:20 p.m.

Rory crept alongside the garage, mindful of the corner he was nearing. Noises up ahead—someone dragging something heavy—meant he wasn't alone.

"This is the police!" Rory drew his gun as he met the corner. He couldn't find the source of the noises in the empty back lot. "I'm going to need whoever is out here to come out with their hands up where I can see them."

The wind was all that replied.

Inside J.J.'s Garage

5:24 p.m.

Irvin was annoyed because it looked like someone was jerking their collective chains. There was nobody here. Prank calls came with the territory on Halloween.

"'Nita, I don't see anyone. Let's leave Cap'n Half-Ass to handle this." Irvin said from across the garage. "There's just a bunch of oil spilled and—wait a minute." He bent down to better inspect the puddle.

"You got something?" Anita asked when he went quiet.

"This ain't oil, it's—" Irvin was saying as an engine block swung from chains suspended from the ceiling. The pitch was perfect, catching him center mass and flinging him through the garage

door into the street.

Anita yelled, firing her gun at the shape in

the rafters.

Her aim was not as good.

Rory walked through the door into the rear of the garage and almost threw up.

There was J.J.'s daughter, her face all mangled, strewn out next to what had once been someone dressed as a priest. Entrails snaked out from the body—minus its head and right arm—as though the holy man had swallowed a stick of dynamite.

As he wretched, double over, something sharp drove through Rory's shoulder from behind.

"Sorry," J.J. said. She left the shard of scrap metal in Rory's shoulder and picked up two acetylene tanks. Her arms were purple, as was her neck and half of her face. "But I've got to get these someplace, and I've no time to wait for your consciousness to become malleable."

Rory desperately tried to pull out the makeshift weapon in his back as someone inside the garage started shooting.

J.J. walked away carrying nearly a quarter-ton hiked up on her shoulders with no more effort than if she were carrying groceries.

Blake & Summers Building

First Floor

7:30 p.m.

"I know I didn't knock you out," Dusty said over the police officer he'd just kicked in the head. He looked at Lauren for confirmation. She nodded. "So get up."

Rory rolled over, the wound in his shoulder causing him to gasp.

"He's really hurt," Lauren said and made to move to Rory.

"We don't have time." Dusty took Lauren by the shoulder and walked her toward the elevator.

"Stop," Rory tried to yell. "Stop right there."

Dusty and Lauren didn't look back.

"It doesn't work," Lauren said about the elevator.

"I figured," Dusty grunted. "You'll have to do it."

Worry shot across Lauren's face.

"You'll be fine," Dusty told her. "I have faith in you."

With a determined grimace, Lauren focused on the elevator doors. Her hands began to shake in the effort, so she placed them in front of her, splaying her fingers apart.

The doors flew open, shattered.

Lauren fell to the floor.

Smoke and debris billowed down the shaft from the floors above. Dusty looked up, squinting through the smoke.

"We're in luck," he said. "The elevator crashed to the bottom. I'll climb us up on these cables. Hop up." He said, turning his back to the young girl.

"I-I don't know if I—" Lauren's eyes teared up.

"Hop up." Dusty waited, his back to her.

Lauren climbed onto his back, and the pair disappeared up the shaft as Rory could only watch.

Blake & Summers Building

Fourth Floor

7:42 p.m.

Eric and Tiffany tried to break out some of the windows on the north side using office chairs but to no avail.

"It's no use," Tiffany said. "These things are probably bulletproof." She dropped the chair.

"We're getting out of here," Eric assured her. "Ayasha's guys' plan is sound."

"Speaking of *my guys*," Ayasha said. "What the hell is taking them so long? Marcus! Christopher! What's our E.T.A. on getting out of this place before it falls down?"

Marcus peeked around the corner of the office where he and Christopher had been working. "Two shakes, I promise! I, erm, *we* could use an extra set of hands in here, though. Just one more of you would do it."

"I'll go," Eric said.

Ayasha and Tiffany sat silently for a moment and then looked at each other.

They both started laughing.

"Can you believe this?" Ayasha asked, drying her eyes. "We finally get a chance to talk, and the world blows up!"

"We are in a building that's *currently on fire*, and I finally feel like my best friend's back." Tiffany smiled.

The elevator doors crinkling apart interrupted their conversation.

"Jesus!" Eric yelled, stopping five feet from the office where he was bound for the creature's embrace.

Dusty stepped out of the elevator shaft, and Lauren slid off his back onto shaky legs.

"Remember, you've got to hold it in place while I perform the ritual," Dusty said as he removed the long, thin blade from the scented cloth.

Lauren shivered. She remembered.

"Who the fuck are you?" Ayasha asked, getting up and walking toward the new arrivals. Tiffany followed behind her.

"Watch out, Ayasha," Eric warned. "Guy's got weapons."

"Did you do this to my studio?" Ayasha yelled. "Try and blow us up like some half-assed terrorist?"

Marcus reached a hand out for Eric, grabbing him by the face.

"Man, get the fu—" Eric's eyes went blank.

"No!" Lauren yelled. Her hands shot up as though she were performing with an invisible marionette. Neon-green energy filled her eyes.

Marcus froze in place. The blood vessels in his hands and face began to burst.

"Hold him!" Dusty yelled, rushing the creature, blade at the ready.

Dark purple energy began to seep from the body of Marcus, flowing into the room like ink in a bucket of water.

"You will not win this day," Marcus' mouth spoke with a voice that was not his. "I will eat your heart, hunter."

Dusty began to slow his advance against his intention as the creature's dark purple energy gripped him.

Lauren's head whipped back as the green energy emanating from her began to fill the room as well, pushing against the creature's dark purple energy.

Nobody else could move as the battle commenced.

"Keep at it!" Dusty ordered Lauren. "Don't you dare ease up!"

"B-but, I can't," Lauren cried. "I'll—"

"DO IT!" Dusty screamed.

A sound like a bomb exploding underwater blasted in the room, and everyone in it fell unconscious.

Paramedics hoisted Eric on a gurney and began transporting him to the makeshift exit. Tiffany had gone ahead of him.

"What do you think was wrong with that little girl?" one firefighter asked another. "She's catatonic. And those eyes! I'm gonna have nightmares."

"You are? What about that bald dude with the funky arms?" his co-conversationalist responded. "His head was spun completely around!"

"Stifle it, you two," another firefighter said. He pointed at Ayasha, who was walking with purpose.

"We need to get you out of her, ma'am," the classier of the firefighters told her.

"One minute," Ayasha said. "I just want to tell my listeners that I'm okay. My guys died so that I could."

She walked into the booth and flipped a switch. A red light suggested power was on, so Ayasha grabbed the mic.

"To everybody listening out there, I just want to say: This is Ayasha After Dark, and I feel amazing! So, on this special Halloween, listen closely. Hear my words. *Lu eribu, wardum*!"

Police Headquarters

Dispatch

9:15 p.m.

Sherie thought this had to be the craziest Halloween night in the town's history. It was chaos! Ranging from property damage to murder. Every cop on duty was out on call, and they'd also started bringing in boots on the ground from County.

"Dispatch," Sherie sighed. She didn't know how much she had in her before she started screaming. "Go ahead."

"Hey, Sherie," Rory's voice came over the radio.

"What do you need, Rory?" Sherie snapped. This guy she didn't need.

"*Lu eribu, wardum*."

It was a phrase that Sherie repeated

throughout the night to every officer whose ear she

had.

Which was all of them.

Imaginary Friend

Henry folded up the packing box and looked around the kitchen. He couldn't help but let a little pride show on his face at having finished. That was the last box. They were finally all moved into their first real house as a family.

Teresa had gone out to pick up some Chinese from a take-out place that one of their new neighbors had mentioned and some celebratory wine for later that evening. Henry imagined that once their daughter Gabriella was asleep, the wine might lead to Teresa and he revisiting the conversation they'd started that morning about christening their new home, surface by surface and in varying degrees of undress.

Henry was pulled out of his daydreaming revelry by Gabriella's voice coming from down the hall. Gabriella was precocious, as four-year-olds can be, and Teresa had mentioned that their little one had seemingly entered the imaginary friend stage of childhood that some kids do. She had heard Gabriella talking to an empty room on more than one occasion since they moved in.

Henry smiled and walked down the hall toward his daughter's room, wishing to see such a precious moment for himself. Gabriella's imagination astounded him sometimes, with the stories she would make up and the questions she would ask. He paused at Gabriella's closed bedroom door and listened.

"I don't have toys like that," she said, matter-of-factly, "but I have a dragon named Hocus that you can play with."

Henry's smile widened.

"No."

Henry thought he could hear some rustling papers, as though maybe Gabriella was coloring with her new friend.

"The girl's my mom, and the boy is my dad."

Henry suppressed a giggle at the cuteness of the situation.

"No, they are nice. They wouldn't do that."

Henry's smile slightly faded.

Gabriella's room beyond the closed door went quiet. Henry began to smell a strange scent through the door.

He quickly opened Gabriella's bedroom door.

His little girl looked up at Henry from what seemed to be pages from a magazine spread out in a small pile around her and smiled at him.

"Hi, Daddy, are you done?" She got up and walked over to Henry, hugging his leg, "Can we play a board game now?"

Henry carefully took a small step back to look down at her. "Gabriella, what is that smell? Did you get into your mother's perfumes again?"

Gabriella's smile folded up into a look that showed she remembered getting into trouble for playing in her mother's things without permission, and she gave Henry a quick "No." Then she tilted her little head to the left and sniffed, followed by a tilt to the right and sniff. "What smell, Daddy?"

Henry sniffed the room, but the smell was gone.

"I—" he sniffed again to be sure, "never mind. I heard you talking to someone, though, and thought—" Henry stopped himself. He didn't know what he'd been thinking or why he'd gotten so unnerved.

"Oh," Gabriella said, "that's the boy who lives here. He plays with me sometimes."

"Gabriella, you know it's just you, me, and Mommy living here." Imaginary friends, to Henry, had suddenly become less precocious than, say, scary. The idea now made him worry about Gabriella's safety.

Gabriella seemed to weigh this statement for a second, her little girl's mind allowing the truth of the situation.

"Well, I guess he used to live here before we did. Maybe he still has a key?"

Henry didn't respond. He was the adult, after all. No need to frighten his daughter with what he felt, particularly since he couldn't explain these sudden scared feelings.

"He lives in our house with his mom. He said his dad used to be here, too, but now he can't find him." Gabriella continued as she dug out the Candyland box from beneath a stack of books and toys, "He told me his mom has bad dreams in the daytime." Again, the feeling of fear crept back over Henry. He looked down at the pages on the floor where Gabriella had been sitting. They were awful images of dead bodies taken from countless magazines and newspapers. All the terrible things humans can do to one another splayed on the floor like a mosaic of horror amidst his daughter's Elmo and favorite Barbie.

"Daddy," Gabriella asked, her face scrunched up quizzically as Henry felt the panic overwhelm him, "how come boys can turn blue?"

*   *   *   *   *

Teresa poured the wine again, refilling first Henry's glass and then her own. Their Chinese food sat untouched on the dining room table, where she'd placed it upon returning home to Henry's stack of death and gore pages.

She sipped her wine. All thoughts of a night of carnal pleasure with her husband, the night's previous intent, had disappeared—the images of death had taken care of that—but seeing Henry so scared when she got home, the story he was telling, had caused her to drink the first glass too quickly.

Her nerves were settling now, and she wanted to keep a clear head.

"Gabriella had these?" Teresa asked as Henry returned from getting their daughter to sleep in their bed.

"It's like I said," Henry began, taking a healthy swig from his wine glass as well, "I heard her talking to someone and went into her room. She was looking at these on the floor when I came in."

"Did she—I mean, is it possible she found them stuffed into one of the closets? Someplace we must've missed when we bought the house?"

Henry took a deep breath and exhaled. He finished his second glass of wine with a gulp. "I dunno. Maybe."

Teresa took another sip of wine, letting her better logic overtake her wilder imaginings. Her rational mind slowly explained away the This Is What You Should Do rules of every crappy horror movie she'd ever seen as nonsense. Henry seemed to be calming down, too.

"Gabriella was just so . . . creepy! The way she nonchalantly asked me about this kid being blue," Henry shivered.

"I thought about that part, too," Teresa said, "and I'd bet you anything it's because we let her watch Avatar with us. Our last night in the apartment, remember?"

Henry smiled and cocked his head back in a sigh. "Avatar! I hadn't even thought of the connection." He finished the wine bottle into his glass as he and Teresa gave over to giggles of relief.

"Kids do that," Teresa laughed, "make those kinds of weird connections in the stories they make up. Pulling stuff from all over the place. If you'd asked her, I bet the boy had a tail." Henry continued to laugh, albeit quietly, to not wake Gabriella. "I mean, I don't blame you," Teresa continued, "for freaking out. Those pictures are awful, and we should throw them out, but I think she just found them somewhere and didn't understand them. We'll talk to her about them in the—"

It was right then that an odor that Henry had first smelled in Gabriella's room overwhelmed the dining room.

"Oh, God," Teresa said, covering her nose from the strong scent, "what is—"

Then, they could hear the water blast from the bathtub faucet from their bedroom down the hall, from the master bath. As the sound, like the bathtub filling, came down the hallway, it hit Henry what the smell was.

What he'd smelled in Gabriella's room earlier.

The overpowering scent now.

It was bubble bath soap.

The kind you use for a child's bath.

"Mommy!" Gabriella screamed at the exact moment that the doors began opening and slamming shut all around the house.

Teresa toppled her chair over, hopping out of it. Henry knocked the table aside as both parents raced down the hall toward their bedroom.

The door was closed. The bathtub filling up was the only sound from behind it.

"Gabriella!" Teresa screamed as Henry tried to kick the door open.

"Teresa," Henry kicked again and again, "it won't—Gabriella!" he pounded on the door.

Silence.

The bedroom door opened.

The room was turned topsy-turvy, anything in it scattered or broken. Henry and Teresa ran in, scouring for any sign of Gabriella amidst the strewn clothes, bedclothes, and broken lamps, only to come up empty-handed.

"Henry," Teresa said, pointing to the closed bathroom door.

The couple went over to the door and turned the handle.

The room inside was filled with steam, but they could each make out Gabriella sitting on the toilet with her legs drawn up to her chest. She was staring toward the bathtub, the shower curtain closed.

"His mommy was so scared," Gabriella said, turning wide-eyed to her parents as Henry ran to her.

"He can't breathe." She said, her eyes brimming with tears.

Teresa crept toward the bathtub.

She drew back the curtain.

__Twelve Days__

There is an intonation, very faint, murmuring in the dark. Voices chanting words that have lacked definition long before the age of man.

Then, nothing.

The First Day

The sound of trickling water stirs me from my stupor, its thirst-quenching promise to my much-maligned throat akin to the cock's crow. I awake to complete darkness, nearly denying my memory of light's existence. As my hands slowly remember their function, I feel through the black for my surroundings.

I am on my back, or so the proximity of the stone floor found by my fingertips would suggest. Yet I cannot be sure how much I can trust my senses right now, shrouded in this womb of pitch as I am. Nevertheless, my sense of hearing stands faithfully at the forefront, as the sound of water is the only constant I have encountered thus far outside of the darkness.

I try to sit up and am instantly overwhelmed by nausea at the idea of doing so. With my head dizzy, I lie here a bit longer and ponder my current state. Try as I may, in the few moments consciousness has awarded me, the search for my recollection of how I have come here has borne no fruit.

It is this that sets the panic in.

How could I not have acknowledged it at once, this sense of self-preservation? I am drugged, cast into a stone pit that not even light can escape! Where am I? I would scream if my throat would allow, for such is my plight that screaming is the only logic my mind leaves me! Help! Please! my face pleads in pained pantomime, though nary a harsh whisper comes forth in the attempt—wet pools well in my eyes.

I sit bolt upright, ignoring vertigo's call to the sick bristling in my stomach, and instantly take a sharp blow to my head. Lost as I am to this darkness, the only evidence I have that consciousness, ever the fickle rogue, is fading is that the sound of running water, my constant companion in this hell, is going quiet.

The Second Day

I awake again due to an intense thirst and a throbbing pain in my forehead. I place my fingers on my brow, digging through my matted hair; a preliminary search to assess the damage. I find it cracked and sticky, the dried blood suggesting I have been out for some time. Thankfully, the drug seems to have worked its way out of my system as my thoughts no longer feel as though whispered to me from across a great hall. The one failing of my sobriety, it seems, is now I notice how cold I am, wearing just my night clothes.

I try to warm myself by rubbing my arms.

I slowly bring my hands back down to my sides, remembering that such movements got me struck when last I woke. My captor must indeed be supernatural to function in such darkness, as my senses have relayed nothing of my surroundings save the trickling of water.

This truly frightens me!

I am suddenly overwhelmed by thoughts of demonic wraiths and other foul, fearsome beasts recalled from the shadows of my childhood nursery. How a billowing curtain, to my child eyes, hid an angry spirit bent on sucking the marrow from my bones. The sound of labored breathing was the only warning one got before the toothy maw of some spawn from hell's pit had its way with you.

But I am being ridiculous. I must try and calm my nerves. Focus on my breathing—steady my heart's pace. Surely I come here by human hands, and if a madman be to blame—for my current state could only have been born of an unhinged mind—I can attempt to contend with a madman. To do so, however, first, I must understand where I am and how I have come here.

Last I recall, I had eaten my meal, retired for the night, or started to do so. I do not remember lying down to bed, however. No, I had gone up the stairs toward my room . . . I think, had I been drinking? I don't believe so . . . and yet I do remember being hauled upstairs. I have no memory of what transpired thereafter. Was I hit? I feel no evidence of it if so. Indeed I was drugged, though, that much I can deduce from my state of mind upon waking here; the lethargic way my body had heeded my commands. No, the only proof of violence that I feel, as I cannot look myself over in such an environment as this to know, is the rawness of my throat and the blow I took to the head after last waking.

Why does my attacker not make himself known? Does he just stand there in the dark, idly waiting for me to move to strike me back down? Lying still like this, I have noticed that my sense of hearing has exceeded its standard capacity, making up for the loss of my other senses' acuteness. I have heard no movement, none. Nothing that would suggest someone is here with me. All I *do* hear is dripping water. It sounds as though it is coming from nearby, and I desperately need a drink.

I slowly run my hands out to either side of my body, feeling the smoothness of the cold stone all around me. It occurs to me that I may be in a cellar, but the fact that I feel no edges in the stone floor suggests otherwise. A cave, perhaps? Surely not. No cave I have ever heard tell of had such smooth, worn surfaces as this, let alone the lack of even the smallest pebble! No, indeed, this must be manmade. My assailant must be quite the craftsman, on top of being undeniably insane, to have created such a place as this. Pity its only function seems to be housing tormented souls for its maker's twisted pleasure.

But enough, my deprived throat demands that water. Perhaps if I move very slowly, crawling on my belly, I can find where the water comes from. I shift no more than an inch sideways. My lower back, buttocks, and thighs groan in anguish at this treatment, having been as still as they have been for so long. I stop and hold my breath. Mainly to see if another blow from my invisible captor is forthcoming, but also to let the stabbing pins and needles in my legs subside.

As my circulation corrects itself and my blood begins to flow freely again, I turn over onto my belly. I quickly put my hands over my head to ward off any crushing blows, but none come. Perhaps it is safe to start crawling now. I listen from which direction the water is coming and gradually pull myself along the stone floor toward it, first with my left hand. Then my right hand. The sound of water is getting louder, getting closer. The stone is freezing; my hands are going numb.

I now feel the gentlest hint of a breeze, barely perceptible on my face and hands. Then, icy water droplets hit me! I quickly jerk forward, and my hands splash into a thin, liquid film that is covering the floor immediately in front of me. The constant nudging from the cracked, sandy pipe that almost certainly resides where my throat had been begs me to drink, and so, like a mistreated hound, I begin lapping up what condensation I can. Thankfully it *is* water. As this merely teases my thirst, I edge forward, licking the floor.

I sense the wall just before I hit it; its smooth, cold surface mirroring that of the floor. As the water trickles down like a small, ice-cold stream, I run my hands along it. I pull my hair out of the way and plant my cheek into the wall, careless of my gashed forehead, and open wide my desperate mouth.

As I lay here, my hair and night shirt absorbing the sound of the dripping as well as the icy cold water itself, I drink deep that which splashes past my parted lips, allowing a respite to my body's tension.

Yet as I relax, my mind, seemingly wishful of relinquishing its grip, cunningly chooses to conjure an image of an ornate, golden chalice resting on a small table. The letters and symbols adorning the cup are unknown to me, as is the mercurial liquid, poured to overflowing by a hidden hand from an unseen source, down its sides.

The image shifts in my mind's eye, and I now see the cup and table from directly above, looking down, instead of, much like a small child would, viewing it from the side, slightly up, as I had been. The silver-hued liquid, which for reasons I cannot say I conclude to be poison, continues to pour over the cup's sides, filling up hidden rivulets carved into the table's surface to reveal a very distinct, very detailed peacock.

Wait, what was that? In the new silence of my prison, I think I heard a faint, almost imperceptible-

Scitter-scritch.

The noise, combined with the odd images of the chalice and the peacock, breaks the vision's hold, and I push away from the wall forcefully, gasping for breath. I quickly crawl away, minding to keep my head low, ever aware of my invisible assailant. The dripping from the water continues again, robbing me of the ability to focus on what I am sure I heard somewhere in the dark. The dampness of my clothes, of my hair, brings on a chill that causes my teeth to chatter uncontrollably, providing any other sounds, other noises, ample hiding ground.

The Third Day

I must have fallen asleep at some point; listening to the darkness, or possibly the intense shock of ice water and cold stone, led to my losing consciousness. Regardless of the how, I have passed out and come to once more; awoken again to the reignited cadence of the dripping water.

A dangerous rumble emits from my stomach; my body responding to the tending of its thirst by complaining of its hunger. I shush another grumble from my belly with a pat, fearful of reminding my seemingly inattentive host of my presence once again, like an older sibling might silence a younger one during mass for fear of a parental reprimand falling on both of their heads.

Along with hunger, I feel weak from the cold. I run my hands under my nightshirt, along my chest and shoulders, to find some semblance of warmth through my convulsive shuddering. It appears to be working, or would if my legs weren't shaking with equal effort. My skin is hot, feverish.

It is possible I imagined the sound earlier. Was it yesterday? It is difficult to discern the passage of time down here. Down here? I find it humorous, my supposition that I am underground. I presume it is due to my hands having adapted to the constant feel of stone, though arguably, it is just as likely that I am in some windowless castle turret. Both scenarios share equal probability when factoring in my life's current turn *bears no logic*!

Enough! It is time I stopped reacting and thought things through. What is the purpose of kidnapping me and putting me here? No demands have been made of me. No questions asked. I have committed no crime to warrant a secret arrest. Let alone forgoing a fair argument or trial of any kind, only to do away with me in some solitary dungeon where one spends their day drinking from the floor and starving to death!

I throw my hand out, punching the air in frustration, only to have it hit stone.

I wince in pain, bringing my hand back quickly. Stone? Did I crawl under some cavernous overhanging while retreating from my imagined noise? I slowly put both hands above my face and extend both arms up only to find that it *was* stone I hit! A rock ceiling! I turn over on my belly, crawl a few feet towards the sound of the water dripping and turn back over. I cautiously reach up again. More smooth rock! I sit up slowly and inspect. The smooth, stone ceiling hangs low, making for a space three-and-a-half feet deep, leaving just enough room to sit with my legs crossed if I bend my head low.

My head!

I had not been hit by a demonic jailer at all but rather bumped my head into the ceiling while sitting up too quickly!

I hurriedly crawl and feel my way around, surveying my surroundings through the dark with my hands. The area is about fifteen feet by fifteen feet, roughly four feet deep—stone throughout. Except for the cracks where the water is trickling in and a few other small holes in one of the other walls, there is no foreseeable way in or out.

No doors. No caverns.

I am sealed in.

The Fourth Day

Somehow, I slept. I dreamed of running through endless marble halls, bombarded by a horrific cacophony of tortured mewling. Yet no respite did my fractured psyche find upon waking in this, my seemingly inexorable domicile. I am left only further disheartened. I understand no part of this; my being here, how I got *to* be here. My fear of a mad captor has turned phantom, replaced by an encroaching presentiment I feel at my soul's edge.

But this is the age of science! In the face of madness such as this, I need only utilize logic and reason to survive. I must recollect my final moments before my first memory of this place. No, not my *final* moments. Not final.

My memory preceding this stone dwelling . . . is . . . well surely I can recall . . . perhaps I am merely thirsty. And hunger gnaws at my ribs like a rabid beast. I cannot force my mind to hunt for memory under such duress.

I move toward the dripping water; I hardly even notice the sound anymore. It has become just another part of my prison, lost in afterthought. Crouching as I am, I laugh, just a little, at how foolish I was upon my arrival here, thinking as I did that some fiend was striking me down in the darkness, bashing my head about in the black.

160

Incredulous! I can only assume it was the drugs in my system slowing my thinking because the idea is laughable to me now. I give a good chuckle at my silly notion, loud enough to catch a faint reverberation of it returned to me from my stone confines.

"Ha!" I test the strength of my voice and find it up to the task. With volume increased above a rasp, the sound of my laughter returns to me tenfold.

I sip from my literal *fons vitæ* to further sluice the damage done to my throat.

"*La existencia de Dios es cognoscible!*"

Mother would feel no small measure of pride that I remember my Gabirol studies, even if Father would not.

"None of the answers I sought were to be

found in the *Summa Theologica*, either, Father."

The memory of telling my parents of my plans to leave the seminary comes unbidden. My mother's tears. My father's barely-contained rage when he asked me to leave his house upon realizing that my mind held fast to a belief in science.

I sip from the cool water again, this time with no hint of mirth. My premature sense of joviality has faded into the darkness.

The Fifth Day

My stomach is distended, and my bladder aches. It occurs to me that I have not expunged any waste from my body in all of the time I have been here. A week or more? Again, my sense of time in this sinister shadow world leaves much to be desired. The drugs used to magic me away must have somehow suppressed my body's essential functions. The need to relieve myself now only adds further credence to my supposition that I am free of the drug's hold.

I painfully crouch-crawl my way to the corner furthest away from my trickling stream, for even the wildest of beasts knows not to despoil its water source. Then, satisfied, I lift my nightshirt over my head. It is colder still without the flimsy garment to shield me, but I have no wish to inadvertently pollute my only resource for warmth.

Clear of my nightshirt, I ease the burden of my bladder and urinate, aiming carefully in the darkness to not wet where I know my knees to be. The urine flows freely, splashing louder than even the dripping of my drinking water. I shimmy my feet in the hope of not finding myself submerged in the puddle I know to be growing toward them. I can feel the heat of my waste and disgust myself by thinking how warm it would be to lie down in it.

Sickened though I am, I must currently focus on the now bordering involuntary pushing of my bowels.

The Sixth Day

I have become desensitized to the smell of myself, my body's stench, and my feces. But, it is more than that. I am forgetting scents in general. The smell of the apple blossoms from the orchard I played in as a child. The smoke from my father's pipe. Roasted duck. Even the stone of this room has no play upon my olfactory passages.

"YEAAARRRGGGH! SPEAK TO ME! WHO IS THERE?!"

I pound at the floor as would a child.

I see dark. My head is spinning, yet all I see

is dark. I am tossed about in a storm with no up or down. I feel my face but am unable to see my hand. Spinning, spinning, spinning.

"London Bridge has fallen down fallen down fallen down, fair Lady."

What is light? Where is my dog? Do the forsaken take to the pubs, or do the pubs gather the forsaken like lost lambs? I am so hungry. I cannot stop my head spinning.

"Wood and clay will wash away, fair Lady, wood and clay will wash away!"

I roll and roll until I hit a wall. Then, I roll and roll the other way until I do the same. I sit up quickly, purposely, so as to hit my head again. The white flash of pain is a pleasant distraction from this blackest night. I feel blood seeping down into my eyes, and it burns. I lie back down on the cold stone.

"Set a man to watch all night, fair Lady. You make him watch and watch and watch, and if he sleeps, you scream SPEAK!!! TELL ME WHAT YOU WANT OF ME!! And then you punish him for his silence and his sin. You punish him, fair lady, and then you build again."

I am breathing hard. My heart is racing, and my head is bleeding. Then, for the briefest hint of a glimpse, I saw white again, and now I can smell my stench once more.

I still feel as though I am spinning on the floor of the cold stone room.

The Seventh Day

Scitter-scritch

It is Christmas time. I think—yes, it is. Christmas was nigh when I was absconded; I am almost sure of it. Has it passed? I have not celebrated in some years. My work keeps me busy. It is important, my work. I will help see to it that we need not be sick one day. We need not suffer.

One day.

I am having a memory. Or a dream. Is it possible to have a dream of a memory? I think that must be what is happening.

It is also Christmas in my dream memory. I am a child lying awake in my bed. I have heard a story, a myth, at school that animals are gifted with the power of speech for one hour at midnight on Christmas Eve, and I lie awake with Gertrude, the family cat, by my side, waiting to find the truth of it.

It is dark in this dream memory of my room, and I stroke Gertrude while she sleeps, trying to relax the notion in my child's mind that I have something to fear from that dark.

This dark.

Wait, no. I am in *that* dark, in my room, stroking Gertrude. I will wake her up at midnight and ask her to speak to me. Gertrude loves me. She will if she can. If she cannot, I will return to school and tell the other children they are wrong. That what they believe to be true is not. They will thank me for my efforts. For is it not better to be right in what you think? What you believe? I think so. And if I am not right in my thinking, I appreciate proof of my wrongness, of my misguided process.

And so I lie and wait for midnight, in the dark. It must be nearly midnight. I am incapable of placing the time here. In my room.

I am a child.

I sleep.

Midnight passes without my consideration.

I wake early, up even before my parents, even before the sun. My nocturnal experiment forgotten, I am excited to open my gifts. Mother does not celebrate Christmas, but she always sees to it that I have presents to open. Wonderfully wrapped presents, with ribbons and bows.

I am a happy child.

Father thinks me spoiled, certainly never more so than at Christmas time. He feels I should be more studious, more aware of the world around me. We will give to the orphanage and work at the church this afternoon, but Christmas morning belongs to me.

I hurry from my covers and toward my bed chamber door. Gertrude meows loudly at the disruption. I slowly open the door and peer out into the hallway. It is still dark. I cannot see the doorway leading to my parents' bed chamber. The silent hallway is unnatural. I feel . . . trepidation.

I turn back to my door, only to be met with more aberrant darkness.

I am not standing outside my bed chamber.

I am not in my father's house on Christmas morning.

I am inexplicably in a stone prison with no doors, left and forgotten to rot for unvoiced reasons.

The Eighth Day

Scitter-scritch.

I awake to discover myself covered in vomit. Or bile, it would seem, since my stomach has had no contents to speak of in some time. I find that I no longer hunger in any way that I understand. My need for food is threatening my life; however, my body can no longer relay that information to my mind properly. The hunger has simply gone beyond my body's capacity to communicate it.

My body aches.

My lips feel damaged past repair. Cracked and dry from malnutrition.

I taste blood from my gums when I swallow.

My circulatory system is in shock, causing my feet and ankles to swell so that it hurts when I move.

I have quit moving.

The entirety of my universe consists of stone, dark, and pain.

And the dripping of the . . . wait.

The water.

I no longer hear the trickle of the water.

When did the water stop dripping? What

could have caused . . .

I contend with the pain of moving and drag myself toward where the water flows. I know the path well by this time. The pain of moving . . . nearly unbearable. Unbearable. That word has little meaning to me now. Words, in general, have little meaning to me now.

I had a cat once. Or was it a dog?

I cannot recall at present.

It will come to me.

But where is the water?

I feel the ice on the ground first as I approach the wall. Somehow I missed the chill in the air, the fact that my prison had frozen while I was focusing on other things. My water supply is now ice. I run my damaged mouth over the ice out of habit. My tongue dances on the icy stalactite as I feel a laugh coming over me. A dangerous laugh. I must bury it deep, my dangerous laughter; for once I give free rein to it, I may never stop it again.

It was Christmas at my father's house.

There were to be presents in beautiful ribbons and bows.

The Ninth Day

"So I tell him, I says '*you* can go down to Cambridge if ya like, but nothin' doin' for this here rat!', and ya knows what he tells me? He tosses that blemished face of his around and says, 'you's a coward you are!'! You imagine it? Callin' *me* out as coward? Nimbi the rat has never known cowardice no how. 'S'just good sense, goin' nowhere near Cambridge Circus come baiting day!"

Scitter-scritch.

"Mf malway sed 'e fwernt wite."

"Now ya mustn't talk so, what with yer mouth all full up, Lil. Whatchoo on about?"

Scitter-scritch.

"Gulp. I said, now you look here, I've always said he weren't right in his ol' scarred noggin."

Scitter-scritch.

"Right so, Lil luv, ya did at that. Couldn't help but notice me pet, that ya still had relations with him 'fore he headed off to his doom."

Scitter-scritch.

"Now Nimbi, don't you go gettin' yourself worked up about none a that. Ain't a bit of your concern who I lay with. A lady, well, she just knows, and he's plannin' on meetin' us here after, so—"

"Silence! What kind of demon voices from the dark—cease your inane prattling, monsters!"

I can take no more. I sit erect, minding my head this time, and scream toward the cockney madness in the shadow. Then, feeling around on the ground before me, I pull myself forward.

"Ya think he hears us, luv?" the voice calling himself Nimbi said.

"I'm thinkin' he does indeed, dearest Nimbi." Lil returned. I hate them, these voices in the dark. But, I shall reach them, and then . . .

"Run for it, Lil; he's on to us over here eatin' his rot!"

So, my phantom noise stands revealed. Rats. I capture the first as it tries to escape over my hand. Out of revulsion, I grab the vile creature by its tail and smash it to the ground. Once, twice, three times.

"Nimbi!"

The second rat sobs for its companion, giving its position away. Quickly I scamper toward it in the black and snatch it up.

"Lemme go now! You just lemme go!"

It bites at my hand, drawing blood, and I bite it back.

Out of anger.

Out of hunger.

I bite back and rip.

I spit its head out, its lifeblood dribbling down my chin.

Oh, how I have missed meat.

I bite into its corpse a second time. A third. I tear its fur with my teeth, trying to get to the meat, swallowing a rib down in the process. I rend and shred until I can suck no more of what I need from its carcass.

I collect the other one from where I left it, thinking as I do so that I was very close in my rough estimate of the amount of time that has elapsed.

It seems to be Christmas Eve.

The Tenth Day

The renewed vigor I felt upon eating my impromptu meal is seemingly short-lived. I almost miss the cockney rats now, forced back into solitude the way I am. I go to lick the ice again. I may break some of it off and let it melt in my mouth. A proper sip of water would do me a world of good.

I see a . . . there is something there, in the dark. No, perhaps not.

I pull at the bottom of the stalactite icicle, trying to collect a piece to suck on. If only I had something with which to hit it. I try my fist but to no avail. Then, finally, some shards break loose, and

I gather them.

There! I . . . no. For a moment, I saw what looked to be a blue-tinted mirror, and then another formed across from it. But now, no, it is just I, here alone.

I lean against the wall and close my eyes, though I cannot say why. The world of my waking judgment is now indiscernible from that of my quiescent eye.

A cough racks my body, bringing blood with it. A shiver overtakes me.

I am sitting at my father's table. He is carving a Christmas goose. Mother is smiling into her kerchief at Father's lack of skill with a blade. I am happy.

"There is no hope for you." my father says to me, staring sternly at the goose.

I notice I am not a child at my family table, though I wish to be.

"How can there be," my mother adds, "when you have never done anything of virtue all your life."

I do not understand. I want to tell them so, make them explain things to me, but I cannot seem to speak. Finally, my father puts the carving utensils down on the table.

"A goose is no good," he tells me.

First, a peacock pattern on some unknown table and now a goose at my father's table? I—nothing makes sense. My mind . . . I do not seem to be able to . . .

"He is all but gone, now." my mother tells my father as she sips from her wine glass.

"Pity, I suppose, but what can be done in the

end? We sent him into the world, and this is what has come of it. They've got him, intent to use him for their means." my father sits down in his chair at the head of the table, wiping his hands clean. "You should have become a priest. Science cannot avail you here. Logic has no meaning for what you are about to witness firsthand."

"Have you given up on the Christmas goose?" my mother sniffs at me, sipping again of her wine. I look down at the butchered bird on the plate in front of me. "I wish you had done so sooner. It *is* how you came to be drugged, after all. Surely you realize by now?"

Something in my mind sparks. I remember . . . a late dinner. Had it been goose? I was working so hard. I did not pay attention.

"Good help is important in an aristocratic

world." my father says.

My manservant, what is his name, the new fellow. I do not—I cannot recall. Are they telling me—have I fallen in with scoundrels and thieves?

"Oh look, he thinks he has it." my mother says, "And yet he does not. Not really. Not all of it."

"No," Father adds, "he has the parts but not the sum."

"And he had been so bright as a child." my mother shared, downing the rest of her wine.

The phantoms of my parents take their leave, then, and I am once again alone in my sad little tomb. Hungry, hurting, and painfully alone.

The Eleventh Day

A dull, repetitive intoning, seeming to reverberate from within the very stone itself, is accosting me now. I know not from whence it comes. Has it always been here? I may have mistaken the sound of chanting for that of running water and have thusly been drinking the hum of men all the while. That seems a foolish endeavor, ingesting an incantation. Little wonder my parents crossed the void to belittle my process.

What is it the chants are saying? I do not recognize the language if it indeed is one.

I open my eyes, surprised to find I had had them closed, and see the blue mirror returned, opened a foot in diameter before me. It does not disappear this time but seems to be slowly opening wider. I lay in wonderment, staring at—yes, not a mirror, but what appears to be much like a ship's porthole. Through it are countless stars, endless, as far as my eyes can see.

I reach out and touch my newfound tear in

reality, testing the validity of it, and find a thin, oily membrane over this, the entrance to infinity. Yet, even in my state, my curious mind wonders . . .

But wait . . .

I . . . the chanting . . . I . . . it bids me—wants me—inside . . . inside with the stars. No . . . not me. It bids the *stars*—that *space*—to enter the stone.

Inside the cell.

Inside with *me*.

I am frightened! I miss the darkness of the stone tomb and want away from these stars, this . . . portal. I attempt to crawl from it. The chanting grows louder. The oily membrane envelops first my hand, then quickly my arm. Try as I may, I cannot pull free!

Chanting. Mind-numbing chanting.

My shoulder jerks inside the portal, my head soon to follow. I struggle to take a breath, unaware if I can breathe in the emptiness. I hear a soft "plop" as I pass through. My torso and legs follow until I am entirely on this side of the portal. I turn back to see the stone room grow smaller as I float into the void. I still hear the chanting from the cell where I thought I would die.

I have no explanation, cannot fathom any conjecture as to how I am—

Wait, what is . . . far away, in that distant corner, I can almost see . . . yes, I am most certain. A black spot amongst the stars. A shadow. Growing . . . bigger.

Something is coming.

Hurry!

I frantically try to move, flailing about, and

yet . . . I am not winded. I . . . I am not breathing! I cannot remember *how* to breathe. I turn back toward the black spot. It is bigger still! I no longer care for the how and why of the matter. I shall try to swim through space. It is some thirty feet toward the stone room. Space is directionless, yet I have pivoted so that I am forced to swim upward for the room. I cannot tell if I am getting closer!

Please!

Wait, there, what is that? A rope of some kind! I grab it or attempt to. I look back over my shoulder as I reach blindly for the rope. The spot is closer still, less of a spot now and more of a—a large mass! It cannot be that big it . . .

I reach again for the rope, kicking my legs for it.

Almost . . .

There! Ha-ha! I have it now! I . . . but it is not a rope. It . . . squishes. I do not care. I pull myself along toward the stone room.

Squish, pull. Squish, pull. Squish, pull.

I look back again. It-it cannot be!

The blackness, there in space, it-it is an eye! An eye as big as—it is unfathomable how gigantic—all of Hell could not hold such a monstrosity!

I turn back to the room and see what I am using to pull myself to safety. A body is tilted up on its side in the stone room. The body—I am using not a rope—no rope—but the guts of this new body to find sanctuary from the Eye.

I do not care.

Squish, pull. Squish. Pull. Squish . . . pull.

My arms. My arms no longer remember

what I was attempting to . . .

Squish.

I happen to look below me, as much as an underneath exists in this vastness. There are . . . teeth. I see row upon row of endless teeth. Could I hide the stone room in a mansion, and that mansion deep in the Earth, and my entire world on a planet ten times Earth's size, I would have no hope of staving off being devoured by those teeth.

I look back to the room as the Eye moves nearer, as the Teeth move closer still, and I see that it is *my* body lying there. I am staring at myself. I am trying to find salvation by way of my innards.

I am no longer a man.

The chanting crescendos, then all is silent.

As the Eye watches from afar, I witness the portal to the stone room disappear. I realize now that I am merely a thought that *remembers* being a man. A remembrance being offered as a sacrifice to the Infinite Beast.

As the Teeth part below me, I cease to remember anything at all.

Day Twelve

Scitter-scritch.

A rat scurries across the cold, stone floor toward the human remains. It momentarily pauses to inspect another rat's head, displayed rather unceremoniously in the center of the room. If it recognizes its fellow beast, it makes little note of it, merely nudging the decapitated head with its own scarred face as it continues for its decomposing feast.

It intends to share with no other rat.

Scitter-scritch.

*   *

*

__Patrons__

Dusty Dean

Ashley Hubbard

Daniel Moler

John Taylor

Victoria Wahlman-Banhart

Thank you so much for your

support!

For more info, go to linktr.ee/aaronconaway

www.ingramcontent.com/pod-product-compliance
Lightning Source LLC
Chambersburg PA
CBHW051957220626
47052CB00004B/976